Tales from Mossy Bottom Farm

THE FLOCK FACTOR

Copyright © 2014 by Aardman Animations Ltd.

First U.S. edition 2014

Library of Congress Catalog Card Number 2013955954
ISBN 978-0-7636-7535-6

14 15 16 17 18 19 BVG 10 9 8 7 6 5 4 3 2 1

Printed in Berryville, VA, U.S.A.

This book was typeset in Manticore.
The illustrations were created digitally.

Candlewick Entertainment
An imprint of Candlewick Press
99 Dover Street, Somerville, Massachusetts 02144

visit us at www.candlewick.com

Tales from Mossy Bottom Farm

THE
FLOCK FACTOR

Martin Howard

illustrated by Andy Janes

CANDLEWICK
ENTERTAINMENT

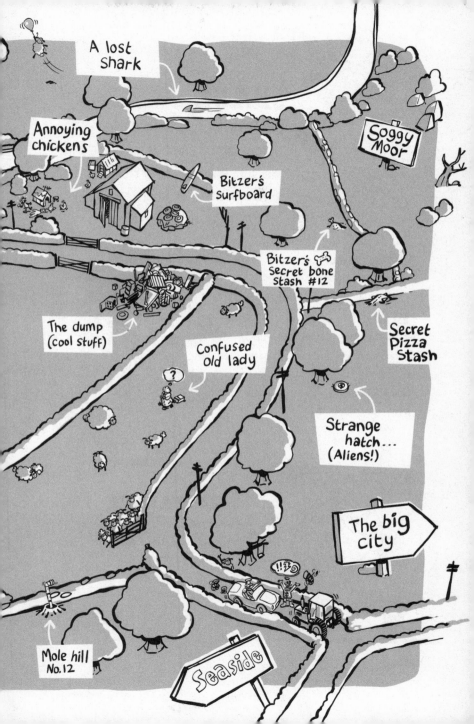

SHAUN is the leader of the flock. He's clever, cool, and always keeps his head, even when the other sheep are losing theirs.

BITZER

The Farmer's faithful dog and a good friend to Shaun, Bitzer is an ever-suffering sheepdog, doing his best to keep Shaun's pals out of trouble.

THE FARMER

Running the farm with Bitzer at his side, the Farmer is completely oblivious to the human-like intelligence — or stupidity — of his flock.

THE FLOCK

One big happy (if slightly dopey) family, the sheep like to play and create mischief together, though it's usually Shaun and Bitzer who sort out the resulting messes.

SHIRLEY

Shirley is an eating machine with a particular fondness for pizza. She's so big that she often gets stuck and needs the other sheep to push, pull, or even slingshot her to safety.

TIMMY

He may be the baby of the flock, but Timmy is often at the center of things. It's a good thing his mum is always there to keep him safe.

TIMMY'S MUM

The very loving, if sometimes absentminded mother of Timmy, she is recognizable by the curlers in her fleece.

CONTENTS

CHAPTER ONE
TA-DA!

Shaun sniffed the stench wafting from the pigsty and leaned against the wall. It was a lovely day on Mossy Bottom Farm, and for once no one was getting into trouble. Well, not serious trouble, he thought as he spotted Mower Mouth the goat munching through one corner of the barn. Exasperated, Shaun nudged Bitzer. The last time the goat had chewed a hole in the barn, pigeons had staged a midnight robbery, stealing wool to line their nests. Poor Nuts had been left almost bald.

Bitzer, however, was lost in music. Eyes shut, he rocked out to the tunes coming from his headphones.

In the meadow, Timmy was tangled up in the string of a kite he had made from a pair of old underpants. Hearing his bleats, Timmy's Mum rushed over and managed to get herself tangled too. Before long they both looked like they'd fallen into a plate of spaghetti.

Chuckling, Shaun nudged Bitzer again. There was goat-chasing, barn-patching, and sheep-untangling to do.

Bitzer opened one eye and sighed. A sheepdog's work was never done.

At that moment, the Farmer opened the farmhouse door. With a loud "Ahhh," he took a lungful of fresh air. After unfolding a creaking deck chair, he slurped a mug of tea and then opened a copy of the *Mossy Bottom Gazette*, grumbling as he scanned the front page. **PARAKEETS IN DISGUISE,** read the headline. Mr. Sweetly had been charged with fraud after selling parakeets disguised as miniature parrots at the village rummage sale.

The Farmer tutted. What was the world coming to?

Suddenly, he sat up straight in his chair. Then, sloshing tea, he jumped to his feet with a loud "Aha!"

Bitzer's and Shaun's heads popped up over the wall. The Farmer's spectacles

Look, a parrot

twinkled with excitement as he peered at the *Mossy Bottom Gazette*. "AHA!" he said again, jabbing the page with a finger. After dropping the newspaper, he hurried into the house.

Shaun's eyes lit up with curiosity. What had the Farmer been reading to make him rush off so quickly? He nudged Bitzer again and pointed.

Bitzer fetched the paper. Shaun pulled it out of his mouth and flicked through a few pages. **PIGEONS STEAL MR. GRAVELLY'S WIG.** He turned the page. **HAVE YOU SEEN THESE PIGEONS?** Underneath were pictures of six identical pigeons. Frowning, Shaun turned another page. "Baaaa" he muttered. This must be it. The newspaper rustled as he and Bitzer leaned closer.

Shaun hid the newspaper as the Farmer returned with two glittering sequined jackets: one gold, one silver. "Hmm," the Farmer muttered, holding up first one, then the other.

After tossing the silver jacket away, he pulled the gold one on over his old sweater. "Ta-da!" he shouted.

Shaun and Bitzer grinned at each other. The Farmer was going to enter the contest! Both of them sniggered. Whenever he took a bath, the Farmer sang like a cow with an upset stomach. And he danced like a pig on roller skates!

The Farmer's antics were attracting attention. One by one, the Flock peeked over the top of the wall. They were joined by curious chickens.

The pigs peered over their wall and pointed as the Farmer fumbled through the pockets of his golden jacket. "Ta-diddly-a-tum-bah-DAH!" he announced, holding up a packet of balloons. He pulled out a pink one and stretched it, giving the rabbits a smile. "Ba-ba-ba-buuuum," he mumbled, pushing one end into his ear.

The rabbits' jaws fell open. Half-eaten carrots dropped to the ground.

The long pink balloon was growing bigger. Red-faced and panting, the Farmer was blowing it up with his ear!

The grin dropped from Shaun's face. He and Bitzer blinked at each other and then stared at the Farmer. He had a talent after all! An amazing talent.

"TA-DAAAA!" the Farmer cried, holding up a balloon model of a small dog. It had a wonky head and only three legs, one of which was twice as long as the others. Or maybe it isn't such an amazing talent after all, Shaun thought.

The rabbits stared, completely bewildered.

The pigs started snickering.

When the Farmer noticed that his model looked like an accident in a sausage factory, he harrumphed, threw it over his shoulder, and stomped back inside.

CHAPTER TWO

~~BEAT~~ IT!
Bleat

The Flock gazed at one another. What on earth was the Farmer up to?

Shaun opened the *Mossy Bottom Gazette* and tapped the page.

The Flock clustered around him. A talent show! Fame! Bright lights, a new barn, some fresh hay, and all the pizza that money could buy! Timmy's Mum was already dreaming of walking down a red carpet. Patting her curlers, she imagined the flashbulbs of a hundred cameras twinkling at her while the crowd called her name. She would have her own perfume, she decided. It would be called **BEAUTY SHEEP: EWE DE TOILETTE BY TIMMY'S MUM.**

Bitzer fell to his knees playing an invisible electric guitar. In his mind, his band, Bitzer and the Bones, rocked out before an audience of thousands of screaming fans.

One of the Twins closed his eyes, picturing himself looking thoughtful and moody on the cover of *Celebrity Sheep* magazine. A hat would be a good idea, he decided. Yes, a hat — with fruit on it.

Every sheep was lost in its dreams of fame, until the peace was shattered by cackling chicken laughter.

The chickens were staring

at Shirley, who was dancing across the meadow. Or was she? Shaun rubbed his eyes. Usually only cake could get Shirley moving, and yet now she was throwing herself around like a leaping tractor. Maybe she has wasps in her wool, Shaun thought. Then Shirley curtsied. It *was* a dance!

The chickens fell on their backs, feet in the air and tears streaming down their beaks.

The smile fell from Shirley's face. With a sob, she hurried away to the barn.

Chickens! Shaun thought. Why do they have to be so cruel? Crossing his front legs, he tapped a hoof at them. If they were so talented, why didn't *they* put on a show?

The chickens went into a huddle, still sniggering. For a while, only a low clucking could be heard, along with the occasional "bu-kiiiirk" of chicken giggling. Then a rooster, chest puffed up, emerged from the group as a hen lifted up a boom box. With a flick of her wing, she hit the play button.

A heavy beat filled the meadow. "Boc-boc-boc-urrrk," rapped the hens, swaying from one foot to the other. The rooster somersaulted. Legs whirling, he landed on a wing tip, then flipped to his feet, bobbing in time with the music. After diving forward, he spun on his beak, then fell into a pose, head resting on one wing tip, legs crossed.

The message was clear: *Beat that!*

Shaun gulped. Uh-oh. He blinked and looked around. Every sheep in the Flock was gaping at the chickens. Bitzer, Shaun noticed, had missed the whole thing. His face screwed up with effort, he was still on his knees performing a guitar solo. The crowd in his head was going wild.

Shaun looked back at the rooster and slowly nodded. He wasn't going to be beaten by a bunch of chickens.

The chickens folded their wings. The rooster crowed scornfully. His meaning was clear: Sheep couldn't perform. When was the last time a sheep had a hit single or sold out a stadium concert? All sheep were good at was looking stupid and eating grass.

Shaun scowled and nodded again decisively. The farm would have its own talent show. Sheep versus chickens. The competition was on.

CHAPTER THREE

ONE TRUE VOICE

Shaun was utterly fed up. Rehearsals were a disaster. The Flock might become famous, but only for being the worst performers since the Magnificent Morris and His Armpit Orchestra. Shaun put his head in his hooves.

Nuts was practicing his farmyard impressions. This turned out to be mostly impressions of sheep. They were good, Shaun had to admit. However, Nuts's other impression was less impressive. Sitting in a bucket of water and saying "Baa" did not make a convincing duck.

Hazel's synchronized frog swimmers were even worse. After flicking out its tongue, one frog caught a fly and swallowed it. It was the first time any of them had moved all day.

Shaun lifted his head and spotted the Sheep-Shape dance troupe going through their moves. Timmy's Mum—dressed in leg warmers and a headband—cartwheeled across the barn and out the door. Bleating at her to stop, the other Sheep-Shape dancers chased her around the meadow.

Shaun frowned as he caught sight of Shirley sitting in a corner of the barn. She was huddled sadly next to a ragged old poster for **BARRY STILES'S SPARKLE CLEAN SHEEP DIP,** watching the acts and blowing her nose. Her dreams of stardom had been

crushed. Shaun's frown turned to a scowl as he remembered the laughing chickens. The Flock *had* to beat them.

The talent show was tomorrow night. Could Shaun create a winning act in time? He rubbed his chin thoughtfully. Would it be cheating to spy on the chickens? Perhaps the rooster's crazy-leg break dancing had been a fluke. Perhaps their other acts would be even worse than the Flock's. There was only one

way to find out. Quickly, he made a pair of
binoculars.

PiPe + Pickle jars

The hedge
has eaten
Shaun!

The chickens' rehearsals were in full
swing. Hunched in a bush, Shaun focused
his binoculars. His heart sank. From what he
could see, the chickens would be presenting
an evening of magical entertainment,
featuring illusion, comedy, and an ultra-cool

rooster boy band. Every act was slick and professional. Who would have guessed that a lifetime of pecking in the dirt could produce such naturally gifted performers? Glumly, Shaun lowered the binoculars and traipsed back across the meadow. The Flock needed a miracle. Desperately, he tried to think up a new act. Something with real showbiz glamour and pizzazz. . . .

Shaun stopped in his tracks.

The most incredible singing he had ever heard was floating through cracks in the barn. A thrilling, powerful voice that made Shaun's fleece stand on end. A voice that was as deep and irresistible as cheese bubbling on a four-cheese pizza. A voice that would absolutely, definitely win any talent show.

Shaun's heart leaped. He waved a hoof at the rest of the Flock. Everyone had to hear this.

The amazing voice even snapped Bitzer out of his rock-star trance. As the sheep crowded around, Bitzer pulled the door to the barn open. He and Shaun peered in. Who could be making such wonderful music?

The barn was empty apart from poor, talentless Shirley, who was writing "Barry + Shirley 4 ever" on the Barry Stiles's Sheep Dip poster. After tiptoeing in, Shaun looked behind a bale of hay. Nothing. Bitzer lifted a bucket. Nothing. He scratched his head. Both of them stared around, bewildered. Surely it couldn't be . . .

Shaun swallowed and pinched himself to make sure he wasn't dreaming. Lost in music and unaware that the Flock was watching her, Shirley gazed up at Barry Stiles, eyes glowing with love, singing her broken heart out.

As the song came to an end, Timmy's Mum was the first to clap her hooves.

Shirley almost jumped out of her fleece. When she saw that the whole Flock was applauding and bleating for an encore, she looked embarrassed and glanced around for somewhere to hide.

Shaun ran to the chalkboard on which he had written the Flock's acts. Grinning, he rubbed out **HAZEL'S FROG SYNCHRONIZED SWIMMING TEAM** and scribbled **SHIRLEY: ONE TRUE VOICE. IN CONCERT!**

He was going to make Shirley a star.

CHAPTER FOUR
CELEBRITY SHEEP

Evening arrived on Mossy Bottom Farm with a glorious sunset, the rubbery screeching sound of balloons being twisted, and the occasional POP followed by grumbled cursing. The Farmer was practicing a new balloon model to wow the talent-show judges. "Gah," he cursed. His balloon donkey was a one-eared beast that looked like it was chewing a wasp. It was clearly a very unhappy donkey. And it only had three legs.

Inside the barn, Shaun bleated at Shirley. She had to go onstage.

For the fifty-third time, she shook her head no. She would rather give up her dream of stardom than be laughed at again.

Shaun was close to despair. Gentle persuasion hadn't worked. Neither had cake, cheese, pineapple on sticks, or a wheelbarrow ride around the meadow. The thought of facing an audience made Shirley tremble like a massive, sheep-shaped jelly. The chickens had ruined her confidence.

Shaun narrowed his eyes, determined. It was up to Shirley's friends to bring her confidence back, and Shaun hadn't given up hope yet. If she felt like a star, surely she would act like one. If only she knew how much she would be adored. Think of all the things she would get at the talent show. . . .

Shaun smiled hopefully.

Shirley clasped her hooves together. She hesitated, nibbling on the cabbages, then shook her head again.

No.

Shaun signaled to Bitzer, who had one last thing to try.

Bitzer passed the latest copy of *Celebrity Sheep* magazine to Shaun. Shaun glanced at Bitzer's work and gave the sheepdog a questioning look. Shuffling his feet, Bitzer grinned and shrugged. He may have gotten carried away with the crayons. Shaun raised an eyebrow at Bitzer and passed the magazine to Shirley.

Shirley's bouquet dropped to the floor as she grabbed the magazine with both hooves, goggling at it. Closing her eyes, she hugged it tightly.

Shaun watched her expectantly.

After opening her eyes, Shirley stared at him, then nodded.

Yes.

CHAPTER FIVE
STARS IN HER EYES

The rooster crowed as the sun came up on the morning of both talent shows. Shaun peered over the wall toward the farmhouse. He chuckled. No matter how many times he watched the Farmer making balloon animals, it never got less funny. This morning, he was purple-faced and blowing up balloons with both ears. In one hand he held a book called *Balloon Animals for Dunces*. In the other was a sad-looking balloon swan with a bent neck, no beak, eight wings, and three legs. With a bad-tempered "Bah! Fahhferrerherrpah," he threw it to the ground and jumped up and down on it. He slammed the door of the farmhouse on his way back inside.

The Farmer was not having a good morning.

Shaun gave the all-clear signal. In the distance, he heard the Peep, peep, peeeeeep of Bitzer's whistle.

Sheep began rolling
rusty oil drums
from the dump
into position
and dropping
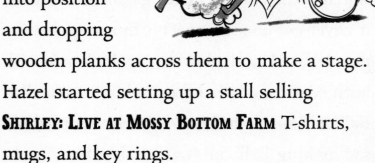
wooden planks across them to make a stage. Hazel started setting up a stall selling **SHIRLEY: LIVE AT MOSSY BOTTOM FARM** T-shirts, mugs, and key rings.

Bitzer, the stage manager, looked down at the list on his clipboard. There was just one word there: Stage. Carefully, he checked it off.

News of the Flock's new act had spread. The hens thought a singing sheep was the most hilarious thing since Bitzer trying (and failing) to walk a tightrope over the manure pile. As Shaun trotted back toward the barn, the rooster laughed until he fell backward off the wall. Shaun carefully shut the barn door behind him. The chickens were in for the biggest shock since they'd found out the ghastly truth about stuffing.

At the far end of the barn, the Twins guarded the **VERY IMPORTANT SHEEP** section, ready to stop any riffraff from bothering the star. Inside the VIS area, Shirley was being a diva and Shaun was worried about time. The competition was in a few hours and Shirley still had to get ready. . . .

36

Sheep-Shape perfected their new dance routine and practiced backing vocals while Hazel tried, once again, to train the frogs. They still didn't look very interested, not even when she showed them their tiny sparkly costumes and swimming caps.

Nuts let out a "Baa" and pulled bales of straw across the barn. His act had taken an exciting new direction since he had added an impression of a tractor.

Meanwhile, behind the sheep's barn, Bitzer's whistle peeped constantly as finishing touches were added to the stage. Moldy shower curtains hung across the front, and a rickety old table had been carried out to make a desk for the judges. It is almost a stage fit for a star, Bitzer thought, admiring his work.

Slowly, the sky darkened. Silhouetted in his bedroom window, the Farmer tweaked his bow tie nervously before stuffing balloons into his pockets. The stars twinkled on his golden jacket as he climbed into the tractor and rattled away toward the Village Hall.

In the barn, the team of sheep around Shirley fell back. She blinked through long false eyelashes made from twigs. Her fleece shone in an enormous cloud, and her head was decorated with leaves and flowers and feathers and parsnips. Her lips and hooves gleamed red. Mossy Bottom Farm's new star twirled as if she could already hear the thunder of applause in her head.

The Flock gasped.

Shirley looked sensational.

And she hardly smelled of cowpats at all.

Shaun grinned: Showtime.

CHAPTER SIX

THE GREATEST SHOW ON MOSSY BOTTOM FARM

The audience took their seats. Tractor headlights blinked on, flooding the stage in light. Bitzer lit an old firework. It fizzed for a second, then fell over. One or two animals clapped slowly until Bitzer held up a paw for silence. It was time to meet . . . THE JUDGES.

A whisper of excitement swept through the crowd. Which glamorous, world-famous celebrities had been flown in especially to judge the Mossy Bottom acts?

Silence fell. The audience held its breath. The curtain pulled back to reveal . . . the moles.

A groan of disappointment went around the audience. None of the moles had even made an effort with glamorous outfits. The three of them peered shortsightedly into the audience through thick spectacles, then shuffled forward and fell off the edge of the stage.

The audience clapped. This was more like it!

Backstage, Shirley bleated nervously while Timmy's Mum made last-minute adjustments to her wool and makeup. Peering around the curtains, Shaun watched Bitzer lean a blackboard against the front of the stage. Tractor headlights picked out the words **EGGY BERYL'S MAGIC.** The first act was about to start.

A cross-looking chicken named Beryl wearing a red fez walked onto the stage.

After bowing to the audience, she tapped her bottom with a magic wand and pulled out an egg. A murmur of amazement ran through the crowd. Beryl bowed again and then held up a nest, turning it this way and that to show the audience that it was empty. After placing it carefully on the stage, she sat on it, waved the wand, clucked irritably, and stood up. Once again, she held up the nest. This time, there was an egg in it. Jaws dropped open. Deafening applause echoed around the meadow.

But Beryl hadn't finished. As a grand finale, she touched one of the moles with her magic bottom and produced another egg, this time from his ear!

The audience hooted and yelled and stamped their feet as the moles held up their scores: an eight, a seven, and . . . another eight. Shaun tutted. It was obvious that the eggs had been hidden under Beryl's fez.

Feeling the ground shudder beneath his hooves, he glanced over his shoulder. The chickens waiting to go onstage were pointing at Shirley and tittering behind their wings. The giggling had made her nervous, and she was shaking so badly the floor was quaking.

Shaun tried waving them away. The chickens just made faces at him.

CRACK!

Next up was Hazel. With a flourish and a deep bow, Bitzer placed a new sign at the front of the stage. It read, **BITZER STAGE MANAGEMENT IS PROUD TO PRESENT HAZEL'S FROG SYNCHRONIZED SWIMMING TEAM.**

To a light sprinkling of applause, Hazel clanked an old metal bucket full of water and frogs onto the stage and hit play on the boom box. As classical music wafted across the meadow, she clasped her hooves in joy. Hazel had had her doubts about the frogs during training. Sometimes she had wondered if they were properly hungry for fame. Once or twice it had seemed that they weren't even paying any attention. Now, when it really mattered, they were performing like stars! The frogs were nothing less than magnificent, weaving beautiful patterns in the bucket and swimming together in a synchronized dance like the unfolding petals of a water lily.

A tear fell from her eye. It was perfect.

The audience was baffled. From below, all they could see was a crying sheep leaning over a bucket. Some started booing and slow clapping. One of the pigs considered throwing a rotten tomato, then thought better of it and ate it instead.

Finally, the music stopped. Hazel took a bow. Her smile faded as two moles held up their scores: zero and zero. Her heart leaped when the last mole held up a ten . . . but only for a moment. After squinting at his scorecard, he realized his mistake and replaced the ten with a zero.

Backstage, chickens wiped tears of laughter from their eyes. Shaun groaned.

Accepting this challenge had been a terrible mistake. What had he been thinking? Chicken laughter would follow the sheep wherever they went, and to make matters worse, Nuts was on soon. Shaun hoped that he hadn't added any more impressions to his act at the last minute.

As Hazel left the stage, Bitzer walked on from the wings, clapping enthusiastically. No one joined in. With a shrug, he swapped the signs. Next up were **CHICKENS CROSSING THE ROAD.**

Shaun crossed his hooves. Maybe the comedy act would be completely and utterly useless.

It wasn't.

Within seconds, the audience was hooting with laughter. Shaun's jaw dropped. Chickens Crossing the Road were telling *sheep* jokes.

51

Still scowling, Shaun patted the trembling Shirley. Her eyes were squeezed closed, as if trying to block the mocking laughter of the chickens from her memory. This time would be far worse. The whole farmyard was watching. If everyone laughed at her, she would never be able to show her face outside the barn again. Except at feeding time, she added to herself. That went without saying.

The chickens were crowing again. Nuts had finished his act and left the stage. Just as Shaun had feared, his farmyard impressions

had not been a smash hit. The moles held up scores: zero, zero, zero. There was just one act to go until Shirley's, and so far the Flock hadn't scored a single point! All hopes now rested on Shirley and her Sheep-Shape backup group.

Bitzer tap-danced onto the stage and changed the sign to **SIX PECK.** Chickens began clucking hysterically, flapping their wings and screeching the names of their favorite Six Peck singers.

The curtain rose. A thumping beat began.

As Six Peck leaped into their dance routine, fans held up homemade signs saying I ❤ Six Peck. A hen who fainted when one of the roosters shook his tail feathers in her direction had to be dragged away by her ankles. Another laid an egg. The air around the barn was filled with squawking, clucking, and the peeping of Bitzer's whistle as he struggled to keep order.

The roosters lapped up the attention. Strutting and parading across the stage, they slipped into their second number as the crowd went crazy. Six Peck skidded across the stage on their knees and did star jumps in perfect time.

As the final beat faded, the audience leaped to their feet, screaming for more. The roosters bowed, then waited as the moles held up their marks: ten, ten, nine. Six Peck strutted offstage, beaks in the air and crowing mockingly as they passed poor, shaking Shirley.

Shirley gulped. Chicken laughter filled the air. Her knees were sagging. Teeth chattering, she shook her head when Shaun told her it was time to go on.

Shaun gave Shirley an encouraging smile.
It was her time to shine. Shirley was petrified.
She couldn't do it! Shaun realized it was time
for some encouragement. . . .

Shirley just shook her head. She was rooted to the spot. She couldn't go onstage. She wouldn't face the laughter.

Desperate, Shaun tried heaving her with his shoulder again. It was no good. Shirley would not be moved.

Six Peck, Beryl, and Chickens Crossing the Road began chuckling again as a tear ran down Shirley's face. Delighted chickens danced from one foot to the other. They were going to win the Mossy Bottom Farm Talent Show. Chickens rule!

Shaun slumped against the wall. It was a disaster. He'd tried everything, and if even cake couldn't tempt Shirley onstage, then nothing could.

Or could it?

Shaun blinked. An idea had struck him. There was one thing that might, just might, give Shirley the confidence to go onstage. Quickly, he whispered in Bitzer's ear, then disappeared into the night.

CHAPTER SEVEN
HIT IT!

The spotlights fell on the stage. The sign read SHIRLEY: ONE ~~TRUE~~ LOUSY VOICE. Underneath, in much smaller letters, were the words, WITH THE ~~AMAZING~~ STUPID SHEEP-SHAPE DANCERS. Backstage, a guilty-looking rooster hid a piece of chalk behind his back.

The audience flapped and cackled. Judges peered at the stage, twiddled their pencils, and whispered to one another. The Sheep-Shape dancers struck a pose, pointing to an empty space with their walking sticks.

Shirley and her one true voice were nowhere to be seen.

The judges shook their heads and scribbled notes. One cleaned his ear out with a pencil.

Still Shirley didn't appear.

Eggy Beryl clucked a cluck full of jeering mockery and scorn. Six Peck put their heads together and crowed a brief bit of "Who's Chicken Now?" And after peering around the curtain, Chickens Crossing the Road wondered aloud if Shirley had gotten lost. Sheep were always too dumb to find the Other Side. Laughter rippled through the audience.

Bitzer ran to the front of the stage and quickly wrote a new sign. It read: **SHIRLEY: ONE TRUE VOICE. WITH VERY SPECIAL GUEST!**

A sheep walked into the spotlights. It wasn't Shirley. The sheep was a stranger to

Mossy Bottom Farm, but he was a sheep everyone knew. They had seen his face on a thousand sacks of sheep dip. He was wearing a sparkly silver jacket. His floppy white hairdo fell over one eye, just like in his picture. When he smiled, his teeth twinkled.

Barry Stiles was here. *He* was the special guest! The crowd went wild.

The star winked at Shirley.

Timmy's Mum checked her curlers and then clasped her front hooves together and fluttered her eyelashes.

Shirley shoved her aside. Barry Stiles held out a hoof to her and smiled a heart-melting smile. His hairdo twitched. Frowning, he shook it back into place, but not before one of Shirley's carrot curlers disappeared into its fluffy depths. There was a munching noise.

Shirley didn't notice. Music bubbled in her heart. She tottered onto the stage to join the Sheep-Shape dancers. Shirley raised a hoof to signal Bitzer:

Hit it!

65

The one true voice was bursting to sing. Eyes squeezed tightly shut, Shirley opened her mouth. Her haunting voice rolled out over the barnyard, plucking at the heart of every animal on the farm as she crooned the theme song to the TV commercial for Barry Stiles's Sheep Dip:

Got a muck-muck-mucky sheep?
Turn it into a luck-luck-lucky sheep!
Don't hesitate. No, don't delay.
Try Barry Stiles's dip today!

Shirley began to dance. Wooden planks bent and groaned. The stage creaked loudly as she leaped into Barry Stiles's arms.

Shirley danced and sang... until ...

CREAK!

CRACK!

CRASH!

And then.....

Silence.

One minute stretched into two.

Barry Stiles's head popped out of the pile of sheep. A gasp rippled through the audience

as his "hairdo" sat up and grabbed what was left of its carrot. Then the "hairdo"—a very ticked-off white rabbit—shook a fist at Barry and hopped away, muttering to itself.

The audience gasped. Barry Stiles was an impostor! Without the disguise, everyone could see that it was, in fact . . . Shaun!

Shaun groaned. Everything had gone horribly—

Shirley's head appeared above the other sheep. She looked around for Barry Stiles and, instead, saw only Shaun in the Farmer's sparkly silver jacket. She folded her front legs. Shaun had better have a very good explanation!

Shaun gave Shirley a sheepish smile. *Sorry* was written all over his face.

Shirley continued to glare and started tapping a hoof too. She was very annoyed.

The sound of clapping broke the silence.

Shaun blinked. What was happening now?

Shirley stared out at the audience. To her surprise, no one was laughing.

Instead, all three judges were on their feet, clapping.

The pigs stood next, whistling and
stamping. One was weeping. He had to use
a hoof to wipe tears from his snout.

Soon the entire audience was on their feet, cheering and squawking and squealing. Wave after wave of applause rang out across Mossy Bottom Farm. Only Six Peck, Chickens Crossing the Road, and Eggy Beryl didn't join in. The rest of the audience was mesmerized.

Shirley stood amid the wreckage of broken wood and torn shower curtains. One of her false eyelashes was hanging off, but the audience didn't care. They cheered even louder when she dropped a curtsy.

And, finally, the moles held up their scorecards: ten, ten, and ten.

It was Shirley's turn to laugh.

Shaun grinned. The one true voice had won the talent contest, after all!

Chapter Eight

VILLAGE HALL VICTORY

Beneath the stars, Shaun and Bitzer leaned against the wall. The Flock was snoring in the barn, the chickens had gone squawking and clucking angrily to the henhouse, and Bitzer had finished his evening rounds. Shaun sighed happily. After all the excitement, he was looking forward to Mossy Bottom Farm getting back to normal—at least for a day or two.

Hearing the familiar roar and rattle of an engine, he squinted into the darkness. In the distance, headlights were approaching. A tractor was coming up the lane, weaving from side to side, its horn honking.

It skidded to a halt outside the farmhouse with something wobbling on its roof. "TA-DAAAA!" roared the Farmer, bounding out of the vehicle and holding a tiny gold cup aloft. "HIP-HIP-HUZZZAHHHH!"

Shaun and Bitzer stared at each other. The Farmer had won the **MOSSY BOTTOM'S GOT TALENT** show! How did that happen?

Bitzer gulped and pointed. Shaun turned to look.

Tied to the roof of the car was a balloon model. It was perfect in every detail and must have used at least a hundred balloons. This time there were no funny faces or missing legs. The Farmer had created balloon art. A life-size model of himself wearing a winged helmet and holding a sword aloft while riding a charging tortoise.

Shaun rolled his eyes, shook his head at Bitzer, and then smiled.

ACTIVITIES

HOW TO DRAW SHAUN

MATERIALS

Pencils

A large sheet of paper

STEP 1 Draw a sausage!

STEP 2 Add eight lines (these are going to be Shaun's legs).

STEP 3 Draw a small oval at the bottom of the front two lines. Repeat for the other six lines, to create Shaun's feet.

STEP 4 Draw an egg shape for Shaun's head. Then add a balloon shape for his tail.

STEP 5 Draw an oval for Shaun's hair and two teardrop shapes for his ears.

STEP 6 Draw circles for Shaun's eyes, and add scalloping to make his wool fluffy. Add some color and shading if you like.

HOW TO MAKE A BALLOON DOG

MATERIALS
A long balloon

STEP 1 Blow the balloon up to about two inches from the end. (Ask a parent or guardian to help you.)

STEP 2 Twist the balloon at points A, B, and C.

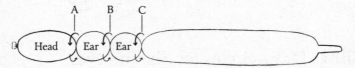

STEP 3 Twist points A and C together.

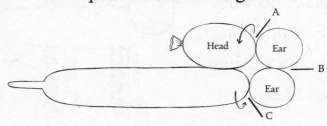

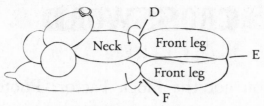

STEP 4 Twist the balloon at points D, E, and F. Then twist points D and F together.

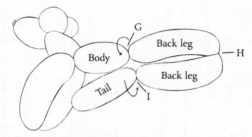

STEP 5 Twist the balloon at points G, H, and I. Then twist points G and I together.

Well done — you've made your first balloon dog!

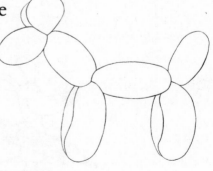

CROSSWORD

Have you got the Flock Factor? Photocopy these pages, then fill in the crossword to find out!

ACROSS

5. Who is the One True Voice?

6. Who does the wig that the pigeons steal belong to?

8. Who are the judges at the Mossy Bottom Farm talent show?

9. What has eight legs, four ears, and no brain?

11. What animals are in Hazel's swimming team?

DOWN

1. What is the Mossy Bottom Farm goat called?

2. Bitzer shows Shirley a copy of: _____ *Sheep* magazine.

3. The farm talent show features a comedy act called _____ Crossing the Road.

4. How many legs does the balloon dog that the Farmer makes have?

5. What is the name of the boy band?

7. What color jacket does the Farmer wear to the talent show?

10. What magically appears in Eggy Beryl's trick?